Silver
Shoes

For Mum and Nan, costume-makers extraordinaire

A Random House Australia book
Published by Random House Australia Pty Ltd
Level 3, 100 Pacific Highway, North Sydney NSW 2060
www.randomhouse.com.au

First published by Random House Australia in 2015

Addresses for companies within the Random House Group can be found at www.randomhouse.com.au/offices

National Library of Australia
Cataloguing-in-Publication Entry

Author: Bound, Samantha-Ellen
Title: And all that jazz
ISBN: 978 0 857982 827 (pbk)
Series: Silver shoes; 1
Target Audience: For primary-school age
Subjects: Dance – Juvenile fiction
Jazz – Juvenile fiction
Dance – Competitions – Juvenile fiction
Dewey Number: A823.4

Cover and internal illustrations by J.Yi
Cover design by Kirby Armstrong
Internal design by Midland Typesetters, Australia
Printed in Australia by Griffin Press, an accredited ISO AS/NZS 14001:2004 Environmental Management System printer

Random House Australia uses papers that are natural, renewable and recyclable products and made from wood grown in sustainable forests. The logging and manufacturing processes are expected to conform to the environmental regulations of the country of origin.

Hit the Streets

SAMANTHA-ELLEN BOUND

RANDOM HOUSE AUSTRALIA

Chapter One

There were two surprises waiting for me at dance class on Wednesday.

Talk about being unprepared.

I walked into class focused – I wanted to show Miss Caroline I'd worked on all the parts of the routine that she said needed attention. Secretly I was hoping the other girls hadn't been practising as much as me – that they might even forget the new moves.

It's not like I wanted them to do badly. I just want to be the best.

When it comes to dancing, you've got to stand out. No one looks at you if you're in the back row.

My name is Eleanor Irvin, but everyone calls me Ellie. I'm ten years old, and dancing is my whole life! Tap, ballet, lyrical – I've tried it all. Ever since I was a toddler. But my all-time favourite style is jazz. When I'm older I'd like to be a famous dancer, or maybe even a choreographer for pop stars. That'd be the coolest job ever.

So when I showed up for class on Wednesday, ready to work hard, the last thing I needed were those two surprises. That really pulled my focus. But another rule of dance is that you have to be adaptable.

I was lacing my new hot-pink jazz sneakers when Miss Caroline called out to the class,

'I know it's short notice, girls, but I've decided to enter a Silver Shoes dance troupe into the Jazz Groove Dance Competition. The competition is only three weeks away, so we have to really work!'

Three weeks! My stomach did a triple aerial right down to the floor. My left foot still had this annoying arch, which totally ruined the line of my legs when I did my grande jeté, and my triple turns were more like two-and-a-half stumbles. How was I going to fix that in three weeks!

And then Miss Caroline dropped in the second surprise.

'Today we also welcome a new dancer to Silver Shoes. Ashley has just moved to Bayside and she knocked our socks off at the audition!'

Miss Caroline makes everyone 'audition' when they come to Silver Shoes so she can see what level we're at, and also if we might be suitable for any competition troupes. Usually it's just a trial class – I don't know why this new girl got her own special audition.

Ashley looked kind of embarrassed and stared down at her shoes, which were tattered old jazz slippers – obviously second-hand. She had short, straight brown hair and kept pushing her fringe out of her eyes.

'What other classes will you be doing at Silver Shoes, Ashley?' asked Miss Caroline.

'I'm hoping to try hip hop,' she said.

Only jazz and hip hop? I thought to myself. She'll never improve if she only takes two classes. Everyone knows you have to be a good all-rounder if you want to get anywhere in dance.

We were all staring at Ashley, but Jasmine and Tove were being super-friendly and waving at her to come over. Their smiles were full of huge, bright white teeth.

Jasmine and Tove are my least favourite people at Silver Shoes. I mean, they're good dancers and pretty or whatever, but that's where the positives end.

Last year I asked Mum if I could get my teeth whitened so my smile could be as shiny as Jasmine's. It looks so good when you're on stage. But Mum put her no-nonsense face on and said, 'One thousand dollars on tooth whitening, Eleanor, or one thousand dollars on dance lessons for this term. You choose.'

I chose dance lessons. Duh. What's the point of getting my teeth whitened if I can't dance to show them off? Gosh, Mum can be silly sometimes.

Anyway, just as I was wondering if Ashley could be a threat to my place in the troupe, Miss Caroline said:

'We'll be auditioning for places in the comp troupe today – I only need eight dancers for what I've got in mind. Let's start warming up. Everyone get ready to bring me your best moves!'

Auditions! Well, that was it for me. I just about died right there.

Chapter Two

Did I tell you? I'm not so good with auditions. I usually try so hard that I end up trying *too* much, and that's when I lose what Miss Caroline says is my 'natural rhythm'. Mum's description of me trying too hard is a 'crazy possessed robot with a bright red face'. I prefer Miss Caroline's spin on it.

I really, really, *really* wanted to get into this competition. I needed to. One, because

people – sometimes important people such as talent scouts – see you at competitions. And two, because if I can't get into one lousy performance troupe in my own dance school, how am I supposed to get into a famous pop star's video clip?

We don't enter competitions very often. And with no eisteddfods or dance festivals coming up on the calendar, if I didn't get into the competition troupe now, I'd be waiting ages to try out for the next one. And, there were almost twenty dancers in our jazz class. Miss Caroline wouldn't even be choosing half.

We all lined up in the studio. My best friend, Paige, was next to me. I felt her looking my way and I knew she wanted to say something, but I was so focused on doing a good job I could barely look at her. She caught my eye in the end, though. Paige always does. It's her best trick.

‘I’m so nervous!’ I whispered.

Paige, whose hair was in a bun so tight it pulled up her eyebrows, smiled at me. Then she gave my foot a squeeze, seeing as it was probably too hard to hug me while she was in the middle of doing the splits.

‘Don’t worry about it, Ellie,’ she said. ‘Just dance like you always do, you’ll be great.’

I couldn’t help but notice she could do a perfect split, while I was still a centimetre off the ground. Ugh. Paige is so perfect sometimes, with her white-blonde curls and big blue eyes. She’s the same height as me but so skinny that her nickname when we were little was Twiggy. It’s lucky she’s my best friend, or I might hate her.

I looked at her split and started to panic but then I realised how silly I was being, and how hard Paige had worked to get the perfect split.

'Focus, Eleanor,' I said to myself. 'You're the best dancer in this class.'

It wasn't quite true. Remember Jasmine, with the big white smile? Well, she's almost as good as me. She might even be better, but only in some areas. Jasmine's always the star in contemporary and classical routines – her flexibility is out of this world. But any style that's upbeat, like jazz or hip hop, those moves belong to me. Jasmine wouldn't be caught dead doing hip hop. She says it's lame. I think it's just because she can't do it that well.

'Good luck, Ellie,' Jasmine said to me now, with her huge, fake, too-white smile.

I stood behind her and made a face at her baby-blue leotard. Ugh, pastels. Bright colours are so much cooler. I'm always embellishing my dance clothes. Back when I had plain black jazz boots, I put pink and silver sparkly laces in them and stuck rhinestones on the top. You have to stand out, even in class. No one wants to look at the same old boring pastels.

Miss Caroline began teaching us the dance. We had to learn it that lesson and perform it for her, so she could pick who was in the dance troupe for Jazz Groove. It was hard, too – she made us do fouettes and axle jumps, and every fourth step seemed like it was a high kick or an attitude.

I was concentrating pretty hard, and I was doing well until I noticed two things that took the pointe right out of my feet.

One was that Jasmine was totally showing off, and Miss Caroline kept beaming at her and saying things like, 'That's it, Jasmine! Perfect!'

The second was that the new girl, Ashley, was really good. She didn't have the best flexibility or technique, but she had great rhythm and style. It was hard to take your eyes off her.

And that's when I fell right on my bum.

Chapter Three

'Ellie! Are you all right?'

Of course Jasmine called out first and made a fuss. Otherwise everyone wouldn't have noticed. (Well, they probably would have, considering I crashed into Riley, who crashed into Jasmine, and then everyone went down like dominoes.) But still, Jasmine was being nasty by drawing attention to my fall.

It was all that new girl Ashley's fault. She'd broken my concentration by showing off and being so good. I scowled at her.

Ashley looked a bit taken aback. But I didn't care. I'd probably ruined my chances at getting into the competition troupe now. To make matters worse, Riley, who was supposed to be one of my closest friends at Silver Shoes, saw me scowling at Ashley. Then Riley flashed *me* a bad look and smiled at Ashley.

Some friend!

'Don't worry about it, Ellie,' said Paige, my *real* friend. She grabbed my arm and helped me up. 'Everybody does it. You just got a bit off balance.'

'Everything all right, Ellie?' asked Miss Caroline. 'Did you hurt yourself?' She stopped the music and the whole class looked at me. My cheeks must have been bright red. I'm

surprised I didn't burn Paige when she helped me up.

'I'm fine,' I said in a small voice.

'I'm not,' said Tove. 'I'm going to have a bruise.'

'I just stumbled a bit, Miss Caroline,' I said. 'I thought the floor was a bit slippery when we were stretching.'

'I didn't notice anything before and I was stretching right where you're standing,' said Jasmine. She flicked her long, caramel-coloured ponytail. 'Maybe your shoes have lost their grip.'

'My shoes are fine,' I snapped at her. 'Maybe you need to *get* a grip.' Then I tossed my own hair and gave Miss Caroline a big smile. 'We can go on now,' I said.

'As long as you're okay,' Miss Caroline said. 'And everyone else. No one needs ice?'

'Ellie needs some for her red face,' Jasmine muttered under her breath.

‘Remember when you fell off the stage last year?’ said Riley to Jasmine. ‘Right in front of Jay, and he saw your knickers.’

Jay teaches hip hop at Silver Shoes. He’s tall and one of the youngest teachers. Jay has this long shaggy haircut that he always flicks to the side when he talks to you. He’s kind of cute.

‘I didn’t fall,’ said Jasmine, her hands on her hips. ‘I was pushed.’

‘If you say so,’ said Riley. She gave me a small smile. I decided she could be my friend again.

I was extra careful not to make any more mistakes while Miss Caroline taught us the rest of the dance. Luckily I hadn’t hurt myself when I fell, but it definitely put me off. I didn’t feel very confident when Miss Caroline asked us to do the final run-through of the dance. I even tried to position myself at the back. I never do that. I'm always front and centre. When Jasmine doesn't steal it from me, of course.

At the end of class we all collapsed on the floor, panting and stretching and anxious to see if we'd made it through. I have to admit, I was kind of sulking at the back. Not even Paige wanted to sit near me.

'You girls are fantastic,' Miss Caroline said. 'And I'd love to see you all in the troupe. Unfortunately I only need eight dancers, but you all handled the choreography well today.'

I love the word 'choreography'. It means putting together the moves for a dance. I've done some choreography myself, for school talent shows. Jasmine calls choreography 'chori'. I hate that. She probably can't say the word properly, so she shortened it to be cool.

'For the competition in three weeks' time I have selected the following people,' Miss Caroline said. 'Jasmine, Riley, Bethany, Tove,

Ashley, Paige, Serah and Eleanor. Well done, girls – be prepared to work hard these next few weeks!'

Oh my god.

I'd been called last.

How disappointing.

How embarrassing.

I'd really messed up.

Chapter Four

My name is never read out last. I was so angry that I'd let myself down.

'You just had a bad day,' Paige told me after we'd taken off our jazz shoes and were walking to the car. 'At least you still got in the troupe.'

'That new girl Ashley got called before me and she hasn't even proven herself yet. She's only been here for one class.'

'She was very good,' said Paige, who never says anything bad about anyone. Even Jasmine.

'I bet Miss Caroline only put Ashley in because she wanted her to feel welcome,' I said sniffily.

'She got in because she's a good dancer,' said Paige. 'And she's funny. I like her.'

'Well, Riley told me she used to go to Dance Art,' I said. Dance Art Academy is our rival dance school. They're this big, rich, posh school in the next suburb. 'So I don't know what she thinks she's doing *here*.'

'Maybe she heard Silver Shoes was the best dance school ever!' Paige grinned.

'Well,' I said, 'fancy Dance Art training or not, she couldn't get her leg very high on the arabesques.' I knew I was being a snot but I had a lot to get off my chest.

'I'm sure that will get straightened out in technique class,' said Paige. She gave me a nudge. 'Hopefully along with your bad mood.'

Paige never calls me out, so I knew I was definitely being a snotty snob. I didn't get a chance to apologise though, because Paige's mum rushed over to us.

'Hiya Paigey, hi Ellie,' she said. Her hair was freshly dyed red and she had lots of sparkly purple eyeshadow on. She looked like the dressing room after a concert. I can't wait until I can wear eye make-up. Mum only lets me when I have a performance.

'You have plenty of time to grow up,' Mum told me, when I tried to wear my false eyelashes to school. 'You don't need to have fluttery eyes to do sums.'

My mum and Paige's mum are very different. Sometimes I don't think my mum likes Mrs Montreal. 'A flapping, gabby parrot,' I overheard her say once, when she thought I couldn't hear. But Mum's always nice to her face.

'How'd you go today, Paigey?' asked Mrs Montreal. 'Did you get those switch leaps we've been working on?'

A switch leap is where you do two splits in the air, switching really fast between the two legs. Hardly anyone in our jazz class can do it. I'm good at pretending, though – it's all in the showmanship.

'Not really,' said Paige. 'We were working on the audition today.'

'Audition?' Paige's mum said immediately, waving her arms around. All the bracelets on her arm jangled. 'What for? Did you get in?'

'Yes,' said Paige. She looked embarrassed.

'Oh, well done!' screamed Mrs Montreal. She swept Paige up in her arms and I almost got knocked out by the tidal wave of perfume that floated after her.

'Thanks,' said Paige, rolling the gravel under her feet.

'Tell me all about it in the car,' said Mrs Montreal. 'See you tomorrow, Ellie!'

'See ya,' I said, and sat down on the church steps to wait for Mum.

Silver Shoes is actually this big old church that Miss Caroline's family had renovated into a dance school. The church was made into two studios and the little church hall out the back was turned into the drama/singing rooms.

They've designed the studios so they're all modern with these huge mirrors and bright lights, but what I like best are the hallways and dressing rooms behind the studios, where they keep the costumes and the props. It's dark and theatrical back there – I love pretending I'm some old-fashioned actress waiting to go on stage.

My mum pulled up late, as usual. She'd just come from teaching class at the gym and she was still in her workout gear with her hair pulled up into a messy ponytail. Unlike Paige's mum, she hardly ever wears make-up, but I think she's just as pretty.

My little brother was in the front seat. He had a bandaid on his knee.

'Hey Lucas,' I said. 'Oh no, did you fall over? You didn't hurt the ground, did you?'

'No,' said Lucas, giggling. 'Got a scratch when I fell off the monkey bars.' His eyes teared up at the memory of it.

'Awesome bandaid,' I said. 'You look like a warrior who's been fighting a dinosaur!' Lucas is obsessed with dinosaurs and swords at the moment, so I really couldn't have told him anything better.

'Rawr!' he said, shaking his moppy blond hair. He swiped his imaginary claws at me and then looked at his knee proudly. I guess that's as good as it gets when you're in prep.

‘I fell over today, too,’ I said. ‘Right on my bum.’

Lucas giggled. Thanks for the sympathy.

‘You all right, love?’ asked Mum. ‘You didn’t hurt yourself?’

‘No,’ I said. ‘It was so embarrassing, though. There’s a new girl who started, too. Her name’s Ashley. She’s really good.’

‘Maybe you can make friends with her?’ suggested Mum.

‘Maybe,’ I said.

But I didn’t mean it. First I had to see how good Ashley was. Silver Shoes was *my* dance school and no one was going to steal my spotlight.

Chapter Five

Technique class was on Thursday, the next day. Technique class is important, but it can also be boring – I'm talking lots of stretching, strengthening, and working on jumps and leaps. But you have to do it if you want to be in the competition troupes.

The hip hop teacher, Jay, also brings in mats and we work on acrobatic skills. I have to admit, I'm not the best at 'tricks'. That's

because I need to work on my flexibility. I practise at home sometimes, but last year I tried to backflip onto my bed, and I broke the plaster on the wall and sprained my toe. I told Mum it was her fault for buying cheap beds, and if I had an expensive one, like Paige, it would have supported me better. But Mum just said: 'There's no support for idiocy.' And then I couldn't dance for a couple of weeks because of my toe.

Geez. A double dose of bad luck and all because I was trying to work on my career. Life is so unfair sometimes.

Technique class is compulsory for every student who wants to be in the competition troupes. You also have to do at least two other classes per week. I do jazz on Wednesdays and lyrical on Saturday mornings. When there's a competition coming up, we also have an extra practice. Miss Caroline says if we're serious about dance, we should be taking classes every day. I've tried to talk to Mum about doing more, but every time I bring it up she has to go prepare for her next class or check her emails or something. You'd think she'd want her daughter to succeed in life, but no.

When Paige and I walked into technique class, I really wanted to make up for falling on my bum yesterday. I noticed Ashley sitting with Riley. Paige and I don't go to the same school as Riley, but we've all been in dance class together since we were tinies. Some people think Riley's a bit snooty, but she's got nothing on Jasmine.

Riley's family is from Fiji – that's so cool, I wish I came from somewhere interesting like that. Sometimes when people ask me I pretend that I'm from America, because that's where all the famous dancers are.

Riley is tall with super long legs and this afro hair that she often wears in two braids. She's an awesome dancer, but I get annoyed with her sometimes. She always gets into performance troupes because she's got great technique, but she misses so many classes because she's on about a hundred sporting teams. I haven't missed one.

'Hey,' said Riley, waving to us. 'You guys remember Ashley?'

Ashley had a hole in the bottom of her tights that had been mended with cotton but started to rip again. She was also missing her ballet flats. 'They're getting resoled,' she said quickly, when I asked about them.

Miss Caroline likes us to look proper in technique class. Remember those boring pastel leotards I was talking about? Well, technique class makes all my worst night-mares come true.

'How come you moved to Bayside?' I asked Ashley.

'My parents got new jobs,' Ashley said.

'What school do you go to?' I asked.

'Bayside Primary,' said Ashley.

'Yuck,' I said. 'Bay*slime* Primary. Why did you come to Silver Shoes?'

Riley started laughing. 'Maybe you should ask her what brand undies she wears as well.'

'I don't wear any,' Ashley said.

Paige looked shocked.

'She's joking, aren't you, Ash?' said Riley.

Ash? What, were they best friends already or something?

'It's not a good idea to go without undies when you're wearing a leotard,' I said, grabbing Paige. 'They go right up your bum and no one wants to see that kind of wedgie.' I hauled on Paige's arm. 'Come on,' I said. 'Let's go warm up.'

'Guys, it was a joke,' Riley said to our backs.

Well, guess what, Riley? Some people don't have time for jokes. *Some* people have their eyes on the prize. *Some* people don't want to get called last for the performance troupe.

I had work to do.

Chapter Six

Miss Caroline called an extra rehearsal every week for the performance troupe. That meant that instead of class on Wednesday and Thursday nights and Saturday mornings, I was now also practising after school on Fridays. I didn't mind. I was in my element.

Miss Caroline taught us the whole dance in one lesson. Does that sound crazy to you? Maybe. But don't forget we *were* the performance troupe. We'd all been in competitions before, and we were the best dancers (for our age group) at Silver Shoes. You'd be surprised at what you can learn in two-and-a-half hours.

The choreography was amazing. Miss Caroline had picked 'You Can't Stop the Beat' from the musical *Hairspray*. It was this fast, bouncy rock and roll music, and it was so upbeat when she first started playing it that we all started dancing on the spot.

I loved the choreography. It was really jazzy and jivey and it also had a bit of swing in it, which I'd seen on one of my favourite dancing reality TV shows. Miss Caroline already had mock costumes to show us – they were these cute tank sleeve dresses, a different colour for each girl, and made out of awesome shimmery material. A couple of layers of tulle made the skirts flare out at the waist.

The dance was fun but hard. Miss Caroline had us doing jazz, swing, partner work and also using a lot of technique for all the lifts and jumps we had to do. Riley and Jasmine absolutely shone at that, of course.

And guess what? Ashley was really good at it, too.

'I did a bit of gymnastics when I was younger, before I started dancing,' she told me, while we were having a water break. 'Then Mum told me I had to pick between the two.'

'Why couldn't you just do both?' I asked.

'Well, I don't want to show everyone up by being good at everything!'

I knew she was just joking around, but I felt like she'd avoided the question. I tried really hard in the dance. My axle jumps might not have been perfect, but I did them, every single time. And when we were doing a swizzle move,

I almost face-planted into the floor. Riley, my partner, started laughing.

'I'm sorry,' she said, 'but you were swinging so hard on my hand.'

'Don't worry about it,' I said. 'Let's just do it again.'

And we did. When I was sure I'd nailed all the choreography, I focused on just having fun with the song, and getting caught up in the energy of the music.

It paid off.

At the end of the class, Miss Caroline told us our positions for the dance. You know where Riley and I were? Yep, right in the middle, up the front. That's the best position for any group dance. Behind us, to either side, were Tove and Jasmine and Bethany and Paige. Ashley and Serah were at the back. I tried not to be too happy about that.

But the best news came after class. As everyone was drifting out, Miss Caroline called me over. 'You worked really hard today, Ellie,' she said. 'I was very impressed with your energy.'

'Thank you, Miss Caroline,' I said. *I bet you regret picking me last*, I thought to myself.

'I'd love for you to do a solo at Jazz Groove,' Miss Caroline said. 'I've got a fun jazz number I think would be perfect for you. Would you like that?'

Do I really need to tell you that I said YES?

But it wasn't until later that I found out Jasmine and Ashley had been given a solo, too.

Chapter Seven

On Saturday after dance class I decided to take ownership of the kitchen.

First I searched the fridge for vegetables. Then I went to the freezer and got out some crumbed fish – it said lemon flavour and I don't really like lemon, but sometimes you gotta make sacrifices. Then I went through the pantry and dragged out all the healthy-looking food I could find.

Mum came in, of course, and ruined it. It was her own fault because she told me she was teaching BodyPump all day at the gym. 'What's burning?' she yelled as she came down the hall. 'Eleanor? What are you up to?'

'What are you up to?' Lucas mimicked behind her.

I was mashing up a banana when she came into the kitchen.

'My god, Eleanor!' she said. 'What are you doing? It looks like a bomb went off in here. Where's your dad?'

'He's in the garden,' I said. 'Not now, Mum.'

'What do you mean, not now?' Mum asked. 'Did he say you could do this?'

'He didn't say I couldn't,' I said.

Mum crossed her arms. 'Eleanor.'

‘I’ve got a dance competition coming up!’ I said. ‘Miss Caroline gave me a solo! I need to be healthy and strong or I won’t win. I heard some of the older girls talking at Silver Shoes this morning. They called this the “Raw Food Diet”, where you only eat raw foods. And it flushes out toxins.’

‘Oh, Eleanor,’ said Mum. ‘You don’t even know what toxins are!’ She screwed up her nose and ran over to the grill, where I was cooking the fish. Well, more like burning it.

‘Eleanor, you can’t cook fish at 280 degrees,’ she said. ‘And a piece of cooked fish isn’t exactly raw food, is it?’

‘I’m not eating raw fish!’ I squealed. ‘Gross!’ I went fishing with my uncle once and I’ll never forget that cold slimy fish looking up at me from the bucket, blood and ooze dribbling from its mouth. Now I can only eat fish if it comes in the finger variety.

'The girls said salmon is the healthiest fish you can eat,' I said. 'We only had these fish fingers, so I used them.'

'Well, they're burnt fingers now,' said Mum, as she switched the grill off and threw the fish in the bin.

'Mum!' I said.

'Look at this mess!' she said.

I looked around. The benchtop was covered in half-chopped vegetables, opened packets of nuts, and jars labelled with names like 'quinoa'. Sure, a lot of the contents were on the bench and not actually in the jars, but it wasn't that bad. Oh, and then there was a puddle around the blender where I'd pressed the wrong setting and the lid had come off instead of mashing up all the ingredients.

Lucas dipped a finger into the mix before Mum could stop him. 'Yuck,' he said. 'Tastes like poo.'

‘How would you know what poo tastes like?’ I said.

‘Eleanor, clean this up,’ said Mum.

‘But I have to eat it!’ I complained.

They were right, though. It really didn’t look nice. And maybe it didn’t taste like poo, but it sure smelled that way.

‘Don’t be a goose,’ Mum said, wiping Lucas’ hands with a towel. ‘You don’t need to go on a silly diet. You’re ten years old. You’re fit and strong as you are, and you eat healthy meals every night for dinner. I should know. I make them myself.’

‘Can we have sausages for tea?’ asked Lucas, as if that was the right moment to be putting in dinner requests.

‘Maybe,’ Mum told him.

‘I’m hungry,’ I said. ‘I have to eat something.’

‘Look,’ said Mum, ‘clean this mess up and I’ll make you some pancakes for lunch.’

Cheater. She knew pancakes were my favourite food.

'I want pancakes!' said Lucas.

'Mum,' I said. 'I'm supposed to be eating *raw* food.'

'I'll put some berries on top,' she said. 'That is, if you haven't used them all in this mess.' She poked around until she found a mixed punnet of strawberries, blueberries and raspberries. 'Success!'

'Success!' mimicked Lucas. 'Pancakes, pancakes!'

'Well?' said Mum. 'Do we have a deal?'

'I guess,' I said, trying not to sound too enthusiastic.

'Go and find your dad,' Mum said. 'Maybe he'll want some as well.'

'I want to find him too!' said Lucas. 'Give me a piggyback, Ellie.'

'Jump on,' I said, and we headed out to look for dad.

I'm not gonna lie, I was kind of relieved. Pancakes sounded a whole lot better than the mush that had been sitting in the blender before me.

Chapter Eight

Do you ever have that feeling when you're exercising so hard you actually start to feel a bit sick? It's like all your lazy parts are hanging out in your throat, ready to come up.

That was me at dance rehearsal.

Miss Caroline was teaching me my solo. She'd choreographed this really high-energy jazz number, sort of cabaret style. I was a cancan dancer, and I had feathers and a hoop

that I had to fit into the routine. I really didn't want to drop the hoop. Imagine if that rolled off the stage and hit one of the judges in the face? How awful. Hopefully if I did drop the hoop it would roll off the stage and trip up Jasmine instead.

The steps in my dance weren't too complicated, but trying to use my props was the tricky part.

'You have a very special energy and a great face for dance, Ellie,' Miss Caroline said. 'And you're very theatrical. When you have a solo where you can act through the steps, you really shine. So in this solo I want to see lots of personality, you've really got to sell the character.'

Pretending that I was someone else added a whole new element to my dancing. I almost forgot my name was Eleanor Irvin and that I had to work so hard now because I fell on my bum in class last week and was about to be upstaged by some new girl with holes in her tights. Instead I was Celeste, star dancer of the Cabaret Club in Paris, and people from all over the world came every night to admire my beautiful dancing and my perfect hoop work.

Towards the end of my solo rehearsal, Miss Caroline got Billie in to have a look at what we'd done. Billie is the Broadway/Musical Theatre teacher at Silver Shoes. I've always wanted to take her classes but Mum's pretty strict with her 'three classes a week' rule.

Billie is cool. She dances in professional musicals all over Australia and she even worked in Asia once, doing a Disney show. She has this funky haircut that she dyes different colours and when she talks to you she always calls you 'lovey' or 'girlfriend'.

Billie danced along with the music as she watched me. She kept yelling out 'More face, more face!' By the end I thought I'd stretched my face so much it had turned into elastic, but Billie clapped and gave me a hug. 'I love it!' she said. 'Brilliant energy and great attack to your moves. You should come take one of my classes sometime, Ellie; we'd love to have you there.'

'But make sure that back leg is straight on your jetés,' said Miss Caroline.

Gosh, that back leg of mine. Sometimes I think it bends just to annoy Miss Caroline.

I thanked them both and headed for the change rooms to get back into my normal clothes. There were all these shimmery shadows coming through the church's stained-glass windows and I felt like they were clapping and cheering for the amazing effort I'd just put in.

I felt great.

I was chasséing past the costume room when who should step out but horse-teeth Jasmine and her little pet pony, Tove. 'Here's a prop for your dance, Ellie,' Jasmine said.

Something flew by my face, but I was caught so unawares that I couldn't catch it. It bounced off my chest and I had to rummage behind the gross dusty heater to fish it out.

It was a red clown nose.

'It's a clown's nose,' said Tove.

No, really? Thanks for that, My Little Pony. I stared at her and thought about how much she looked like a meerkat.

'Because obviously with that dance,' said Jasmine very sweetly, 'you're just clowning around. You'll never win. Why don't you leave the real dancing to the experts?'

'Oh sorry, where will I find those?' I said, looking around everywhere but at Jasmine and Tove.

'She means us,' said Tove. I really didn't think Tove was having a bright day.

'Well,' I said, just as sweetly to Jasmine, 'you do know that clowns are fan favourites. They win everybody's hearts. Takes a lot of skill to look like you're messing everything up.' I made my smile bigger. 'You would know.'

And then, because I knew that the stupid clown nose was meant to freak me out, I reached up and put it on. Then I waved at Jasmine and Tove in a really exaggerated manner, bowed, and went on my merry way to the change rooms.

Gosh. Those two should really stick to munching hay and leave the insults to those who can actually pull them off.

Chapter Nine

Mum was teaching yoga on Friday night, and Dad was with Lucas at some birthday party, so I had to hang around at Silver Shoes after class until Mum could pick me up.

'I can get a lift home with one of the other girls,' I said earlier that day.

'No, no,' said Mum, 'I'll come and get you. We can go somewhere for dinner to celebrate all the hard work you've been doing lately.'

'We can celebrate after I win first place in my solo,' I said. 'I don't want to jinx it.'

'Not everything is about winning,' said Mum.

'It is,' I said. 'Remember when you got chosen to teach that new boxing class at the gym instead of that Donna lady you hate? I saw you dancing around the lounge to celebrate.'

'You shouldn't spy on people, Ellie,' said Mum.

'The lounge room doesn't have a door,' I said, then Mum told me not to be cheeky and that the conversation was closed – which only proved that she liked to win, whether it was a gym class or an argument.

I wished Mum would hurry up – I was starving. Silver Shoes was nice at this time, though. There weren't many girls around, only those who had solo or duo rehearsals, and the

halls were silent and shadowy. If I looked into the rooms, it felt like I'd caught them in the middle of a secret.

Eventually I got bored of pretending someone was chasing me through the dark corridors, and I wandered down towards the church hall, where the singing and drama classes were held. It didn't sound like anyone was doing either of those things, though. The music coming from the half-open door was deep and dramatic, and sounded like someone was dancing the tango.

I peered around the door. Someone *was* dancing the tango.

Someone called my best friend, Paige.

With a boy.

I didn't recognise him. I hoped he wasn't from an enemy studio, and he was here using *our* facilities. He and Paige were standing in front of the mirror in a tango stance – his arms were straight and strong and Miss Caroline would have jumped for joy over the nice lines he created through his shoulders and back.

Paige had her 'I don't want to' face on. She was leaning away from him and stumbling over her own feet as her mum and another lady coached her and the boy around the room.

'Smoother, Paige, smoother,' the lady called out. 'See how Benji moves as though he's connected to the floor? Try to move like him.'

Paige looked like the only thing she wanted to be connected to was a speeding car right out of there.

I had a bad feeling in my gut, like the moment before you forget a step on stage and the whole dance runs through your head in a split second but you can't for the life of you think of what comes next.

Paige was getting *even more* dance lessons. And she'd kept it a secret from me! Here she was, dancing with this boy in *our* Silver Shoes studios, sneaking around. Did that mean she was no longer going to be my duo partner? Had she dumped me for this Benji boy? As if I didn't have enough to worry about, with Jasmine and Ashley and the jazz competition coming up – now I had to worry about my best friend keeping secrets from me?

I made a face at her, which was kind of useless, because I was peeping through the gap in the door and no one saw it, but it made me feel better.

Then I felt worse. Because when I turned to stomp off, there was Ashley, lurking in the halls behind me!

Ashley saw my face. At least it hadn't been a complete waste, then. 'They've been practising a few nights a week,' she said. 'I think they're going to be ballroom partners.'

'Paige doesn't do ballroom,' I snapped.

Ashley shrugged and looked at the studio, like it wasn't obvious what I'd just seen Paige doing.

'What are you doing lurking around anyway?' I said. 'Are you spying for Dance Art?'

'Of course not,' said Ashley. 'I have to wait here until my sister picks me up, and she doesn't finish till six.'

'Don't you have parents?' I said, in what Mum would call my 'peevish' tone.

Ashley shrugged again. 'They work until late, too.'

'Oh,' was all I could think to say. I started picking at the paint on the wall.

'I think Paige's mum is making her do it,' said Ashley, giving me a small smile. 'The ballroom stuff.'

I knew she was trying to make me feel better, but instead I got angry. I didn't need some new girl from Dance Art trying to tell me all about my best friend.

'If you really want to dance, nobody makes you do anything,' I said, tearing at the paint.

A big hunk of it came away in my fingers, revealing faded flowery wallpaper underneath. I looked at it in shock. Great. Now, to add to everything else, I was going to be accused of vandalising my own dance school.

'Don't worry,' said Ashley, grinning. 'If anyone asks, I'll just say I saw Jasmine hanging around here.'

I didn't grin back. 'Okay,' I said. 'Well, whatever. My mum's waiting so I've gotta go. Bye.'

The bad feeling in my gut got worse when I walked away after being mean to Ashley. But the bad feeling in my heart, knowing that Paige had kept secrets from me, was worse.

Chapter Ten

In the week before the competition, I walked into the change rooms at Silver Shoes and there were Riley, Paige and Ashley sitting in one corner, chatting and eating a bag of dried apples.

'Oh, hey,' I said, going to them and helping myself to a big handful. I was being over-confident, I guess, because I felt a little left out and I didn't want the others to see. But then

I saw how much my piggy manners shocked Paige.

'Sorry,' I said. 'I'm starved. Whose are they?'

'Mine,' said Ashley.

Great.

'Sorry,' I said again. 'I don't usually barge in and help myself to food.'

'That's fine,' she said. 'You look hungry. Better the apples than me.'

I saw a sneaky smile flicker at the corner of Riley's mouth.

'How's your solo coming along?' I asked Ashley.

'Really good,' said Ashley. 'It was nice of Miss Caroline to give me one.'

'Yes,' I said, 'it was.'

'I saw Ash rehearsing yesterday,' said Riley. 'Very Beyoncé.'

'I don't really like Beyoncé's dancing,' I said, which was a lie.

'Is Silver Shoes much different to Dance Art?' asked Paige.

'Very,' said Ashley. 'It's a lot more relaxed here.'

'You don't really come to dance class to relax,' I said.

'No,' said Ashley, 'I meant, like, the feel of the place. It's easy to have fun here. You always dance better when you're relaxed and having fun.'

'You're so right,' said Paige.

The dried apples turned to cardboard in my mouth.

'Anyway,' I said, 'I'm going to warm up. It won't be very relaxing if I pull a muscle when I'm having all that fun.'

'I'll come with you,' said Paige. She gave Ashley one of her sweet Paige smiles. 'Thanks for the apples.'

'That's cool,' said Ashley.

Huh. Apples. It's not even tasty junk food. I decided that next week I would bring in a big

jar of snakes, like what we normally snacked on before class, before Ashley poked her nose in. We'll see how much the girls remembered bland dried apples then.

'Are you okay?' asked Paige as we walked out into the second studio.

'Of course,' I said, flicking imaginary dust off my dance tights.

She gave me a hug. 'Just in case you're not.'

For a minute I didn't want her to let go because it made my heart feel big and lovely, and her baby-powder Paige smell was very comforting. But then I remembered about her secret dance life and shrugged the hug off.

I attached my hand to the barre and began swinging my leg back and forth. 'All I want is to do well at the competition.' I did a few more swings. 'It will be so embarrassing if the new girl beats me in my favourite style.'

'At least you got a solo,' said Paige. She was fiddling with her cross-over, tying and untying the knot. When I tried to catch her eye in the mirror she wouldn't look back at me.

'Well, jazz isn't really your best style, Paige,' I said. 'Maybe if we were doing lyrical you would have got it. You're better than almost everyone at lyrical. Or tap. Or even . . . ballroom.'

Paige went as pink as my jazz boots.

'Wh . . . what?' she stammered.

'I saw you practising, Paige,' I said. 'I don't know why you had to keep it a secret from me.'

'I don't want to,' whispered Paige. 'But Mum wants me to enter . . . she picked Benji for me, so we can, you know, like she used to . . . the dancesport stuff.'

The other girls started to trickle into the studio so I didn't say any more. I could see

Paige holding her head like she does when she's trying not to cry.

That made me want to cry. I knew the ballroom was probably her mum's idea. Mrs Montreal used to be a professional ballroom dancer; you should see the huge pictures of herself she has everywhere in Paige's house. I guess when I'd seen Paige practising in secret, I'd been hurt but also a little . . . jealous? Worried? I wish I could take ten different classes a week so *my* dancing could improve too, but Mum seems to think that paying for silly things like bread and milk and petrol is more important. I mean, geez, I could go without sandwiches for a week.

'I'm sorry,' I whispered to Paige. 'I just don't want to lose my duo partner! We're such a good match!'

She gave me a trembly smile, and then class started.

Riley raised her hand. 'Miss Caroline,' she said, 'I have to leave early this afternoon; I have a basketball game tonight.'

Miss Caroline pursed her lips but didn't say anything.

'We have a big competition in less than two weeks,' said Jasmine. 'No one should be leaving early.' She glared at Riley and raised her chin in this snooty way that made her look like an angry emu.

'No one,' echoed Tove.

'That's enough, girls,' said Miss Caroline briskly. 'That's fine, Riley, but you'll need to come in early on Saturday to make up for what you missed today.'

'My brother plays football early –' Riley began, but then closed her mouth when she saw Miss Caroline's face. 'Okay,' she said.

'Very well,' said Miss Caroline. 'You may leave, but do it quietly so you don't disturb the class.'

‘That wouldn’t happen at Dance Art,’ said Jasmine. ‘Would it, Ashley? No one’s allowed to leave early. My cousin goes there and she said it’s really strict.’

Ashley shuffled her feet while Jasmine waited for a reply.

‘Well, that was an interesting answer,’ said Jasmine, turning around to swap mean glances with Tove.

‘So interesting,’ said Tove.

‘The front’s that way,’ said Riley, pointing.

‘You mean where I always stand,’ said Jasmine, acting surprised. ‘And not at the back, where you are?’

‘All the better to see you with, my dear,’ said Riley. Ashley giggled.

‘Very funny,’ snapped Jasmine, narrowing her eyes at Ashley. Someone had just made a new enemy.

While Miss Caroline was lecturing the girls on the importance of refined manners in class, two small hands wrapped around my arm.

'You won't lose me as a duo partner, Ellie,' Paige whispered. 'I love dancing with you. I'm sorry I kept it a secret. I guess I was embarrassed. Mum makes me do all these things and sometimes I just don't want to.'

'Don't worry about it,' I whispered back.

I didn't want to stay mad at Paige, anyway. It takes so much energy to be mad at someone, much more than just being their friend. And I needed all my energy if I was going to win Jazz Groove.

Chapter Eleven

Costume-fitting time! One of my favourite parts of competitions, eisteddfods, concerts and shows. Sometimes when Mum is grocery shopping I even sneak into the material store, just so I can plan out my future costumes with all the new fabrics.

When I'm famous I'd like to have a special room filled with every single costume I've ever worn. People will come from everywhere to look at them. As it is, I keep all my costumes shoved to one side of my wardrobe and Mum always complains that there's not enough room for my school blazers. Priorities, Mum.

We were all piled around the costume room on Thursday, waiting for our turn to be fitted. I poked my head inside and there were measuring tapes and sequins and hair ribbons flying everywhere. Paige's mum was in there with pins in her mouth. She looked extremely happy – Paige is lucky, Mrs Montreal really loves helping out at Silver Shoes.

'Looks pretty crazy in there,' said Ashley, peering around me.

'Yep,' I said.

'So different from Dance Art,' she said. 'We used to have set appointments where we would come in and get fitted.'

'Well, why don't you go back there if you miss it so much,' I said.

'I didn't say I liked it,' said Ashley. She stepped back and tightened the ribbon in her hair. 'It's nice here. I'm really enjoying the classes.'

'Your turn, Ellie,' said Mrs Montreal.

'That's nice,' I said to Ashley. I left her standing at the door. I felt a bit bad, but her new best friend Riley would probably come along soon.

'I don't want purple,' Jasmine was saying to her mum, who was also in charge of making the group costumes for our age group. Mrs de Lacy was holding a purple dress with the most fantastic layers of creamy tulle.

'But it goes with your royal personality,' I said to Jasmine. *Royally snobby*, I added to myself.

'You've got pink, Ellie,' said Mrs Montreal, wrapping the measuring tape around my waist.

'My favourite!' I exclaimed. 'Thank you!'

Pink is my favourite colour. I saw Jasmine eyeing off my dress and knew what was coming.

'Can I have the pink this time?' Jasmine asked. 'Ellie always gets pink.'

'That's a good idea,' said Mrs de Lacy.

'Oh no, it's already done now,' said Mrs Montreal. 'Stand up straight, Elle-belle, so I can see where to take it in.'

'It would be a nice change,' said Mrs de Lacy. 'Eleanor does always get to wear pink. Wouldn't you like to be different for once, Eleanor?'

'I like pink,' I said. 'It makes me dance better.'

'Nonsense,' said Mrs de Lacy.

'Oh, let Ellie have the pink dress,' Mrs Montreal said. 'It isn't hurting anyone.'

'I don't want purple!' Jasmine whined. 'It makes me look like a grape!'

The two mothers stood at either end of the costume room, tulle in their hands. It was like the great dressing room showdown. And there was no way I was going to give up that pink.

'Mum's already made pink hair accessories,' I said, 'so I have to wear the pink or it won't match.' Mum hadn't done any such thing.

'There are hundreds of purple hair accessories around here,' said Jasmine, pointing to the overstuffed boxes. 'I'm sure you could find something if we swapped.'

'I don't want to swap,' I said. 'Mum's already made stuff. It would be rude if I didn't use it.' I was getting upset. The past few weeks had been hard and I didn't need Jasmine being sulky about what colour dress she got to wear. Besides, everyone knows I always wear pink. It's my thing.

Luckily Ashley walked in then. 'I'll wear the purple dress if you like,' she told Jasmine.

'My dress is blue. I heard you say that was your favourite colour the other week. I don't mind swapping.'

Jasmine stared at Ashley. Jasmine's mum stared at Ashley. Ashley grinned at me. I flashed her a small smile but then I quickly looked away.

'This dress was too big for me anyway,' Ashley said, holding out the blue dress. 'But it would look great on you, Jasmine, because you're so tall.'

Too bad, Jas-mean. There was no way she could say no, now.

'Thanks,' she finally said to Ashley, grabbing the dress. But her face wasn't thankful at all. 'Pink clashes with your red hair,' Jasmine hissed at me as we walked out.

'It's strawberry-blonde,' I said.

Some people are just really bad losers.

Chapter Twelve

Mum always comes into my room at the most inappropriate moments.

'Eleanor Irvin!' she said. 'What on earth do you think you're doing?'

I was balancing on my elbows with my head tucked between my knees, so I guess it was a fair question.

'The bird pose, Mum,' I said. And then, because my concentration was broken,

I tipped over. 'Now look what you've done!'

Lucas came barrelling up behind her. 'Squawk, squawk!' he yelled, running in and diving on top of me.

'Squawk, squawk!' I said back, and lifted him up on my feet.

'Why do you feel the need to pose like a bird?' asked Mum.

'I'm meditating,' I told her over Lucas' squeals. 'For peace of mind.'

'Ellie, you're ten years old,' Mum said. 'What could possibly be on your mind?'

'The dance competition!' I blurted. 'It's three days away! I'm not ready! What if I mess up?'

'What have I told you about lighting candles in your room?' Mum huffed, charging around and putting them out. All my peace of mind disappeared in puffs of lavender-scented smoke.

'MUM!'

'A dance competition is not a matter of life or death,' said Mum. 'Nor is it reason to burn the house down.'

'It IS life or death!'

'Don't be a drama queen,' said Mum. 'You'll be wonderful, like you always are. Now come out into the lounge room.'

'No,' I sulked.

'Okay,' said Mum, gathering Lucas up. 'But then I guess you won't see what I've got for you.'

I waited for at least one minute before I followed her. I just couldn't last any longer, because I had a big idea about why Mum wanted me to come out.

I was right.

My brand new solo costume hung over the chair. It was the most beautiful thing I'd ever seen.

Mum had made a black sparkly top that looked like a corset, and all over the shoulders and down the front in a V shape were feathers mixed with spangly jewels. The bottom was black sparkly shorts but covered in the same hot pink feathers, and the feathers got bigger and bigger until they ended in a swirly tail, kind of like a peacock. There was also an amazing jewel and feather arrangement for my hair.

'Mum!' I yelled. 'I love it!'

Of course I had to try it on straightaway. And when I did, it was like stepping into the skin of Celeste, famous cabaret dancer, who had stolen the entire world's hearts.

And I knew I could do it. I knew I could win the competition.

***

I was in such a good mood when I went to my next solo rehearsal.

'Hi Mrs de Lacy,' I said to Jasmine's mum as I walked past reception. 'Hi Jasmine,' I said, as sweet as can be, as I walked past her practising in the big dressing room. She looked like a codfish had slapped her in the face.

'Miss Caroline, Miss Caroline!' I cried, running into the small studio. 'I have my costume – look! It's amazing!'

Miss Caroline held it up. 'Perfect!' she declared.

'I will be!' I replied.

'Well, this is your last rehearsal,' she said, 'so I hope so!'

But nothing could have stopped me now.

My side split leaps had never been higher. Miss Caroline didn't even have to yell out at me to straighten my knees. The lines I created with my arms and feet were worthy of a famous ballerina. I didn't even have to think about which expressions to use – everything came naturally. Even my travelling fouette turns, which I sometimes have trouble with, I breezed right through. A fouette is when you spin on the spot numerous times, using one leg to propel you. Often I throw my leg too hard and end up off balance, but not today. They were slightly easier because Miss Caroline wanted me to travel, and you usually stay on the spot.

At the end of the rehearsal Miss Caroline gave me a hug and said, 'Now there's the Ellie I know. Dance just like that at Jazz Groove and you'll be unstoppable!'

I couldn't wait until I took to the stage.

Chapter Thirteen

For the fifth time, I did a double pirouette, grabbed for Riley, and using her left side for support, hauled myself into the air and did a side split kick. Before I'd even touched the ground, Miss Caroline was calling out:

'No, no, do it again, girls! It wasn't together! Bethany, your kick wasn't high enough; it was twenty centimetres below the other girls'!'

'Sorry, Miss Caroline,' said Bethany.

'Don't be sorry, just do it again,' said Miss Caroline.

Final rehearsal really brings out the drill sergeant in Miss Caroline. I know it's for our own good, and it's what makes us win, but when you've been told ten times that what you're doing isn't good enough, it kind of puts a little crack into your heart.

Luckily we all love Miss Caroline. We all want to do our best for her. And she isn't a drill sergeant for long. After we did the dance again and Bethany got her leg high enough, we had a break for a few minutes. Paige handed out lolly snakes while we caught our breath and forgot that only seconds ago Miss Caroline had been yelling orders at our faces.

You know what? Even now, all sweaty and tired and emotional, I was having the time of my life. Because I knew I'd worked hard doing something I love, and it was the best feeling. And who cared if it was only for a four-minute dance?

Let me explain: once, when I was staying at Nan's, and I was a bit bored because I'd read all her magazines, I pulled down this big, leather poetry book with these awesome old illustrations, and I began flicking through it. It wasn't very interesting, and the language was weird and hard to understand, but there was one poem that went like this:

To see a World in a Grain of Sand
And a Heaven in a Wild Flower,
Hold Infinity in the palm of your hand
And Eternity in an hour.

And I ran out to the kitchen yelling, 'Nan, Nan, this is about dance!'

After she'd gotten over being annoyed because I woke up Toby, her fat grumpy cat, Nan said that was very clever and a beautiful way to think about dancing. Later she even stitched me a picture of a dancer with those words written on the side.

Sure, a dance can only go for a few minutes, but you create a bit of magic in that time. The dance has these little fingers that go reaching out to find all the little happys that make the one big happy – one tiny moment that's somehow full of these unrelated good things.

That sounds dumb, I guess. But the feeling dancing gives me makes all the bad stuff – the mean teachers, the blisters, the leotard wedgies, the annoying Jas-means, the 'I'm about to spew, I pushed too hard' – totally worth it.

After we'd had our share of jelly snakes (I saw Jasmine sneaking extra, even though she says she only eats 'healthy' things), we lined up again and the list went on: point your toes; extend your middle finger; get those arabesques in line with your hip; Ellie, what was that cartwheel doing; liven up your eyes, girls; Serah, get your mum to take in the waist of your dress before competition; maintain the turn-out in your turns; I need more height in that jump!

Finally, *finally*, Miss Caroline was impressed enough to say we were ready for the competition. All of us collapsed on the floor with our hearts jumping up near the roof.

Miss Caroline came around and handed out bottles of water. 'I'm so proud of you, girls,' she said. 'I must have the best young dancers in the world!'

And when I looked over at Ashley, she had the biggest smile on her face. It was like she'd gone to dancing heaven.

I didn't want to believe anyone could like dancing more than me.

Chapter Fourteen

It's so exciting when you arrive at the performance venue for the first time. The Jazz Groove Dance Competition was held at the Two Palms Function Centre. It was a stuffy-looking building with lots of ramps and platforms – it looked more like a council building than a place where you'd dance.

Dance competitions aren't always held in places like Two Palms. Often they're in proper performance theatres or arts centres. A lot of them are held at town halls or in high schools that have really nice performance spaces. Once I even went to a comp that was held in a basketball stadium. It smelled like day-old hot chips and sweaty socks.

The Two Palms Function Centre was an hour's drive away from Silver Shoes. Once you got around to the back, it stopped looking so much like a council building. There was a smallish auditorium (where the audience sits) and a cute stage that had giant white columns either side.

It looked like the perfect place to win a jazz championship.

Miss Caroline and Jay the hip hop teacher herded us around to the side entrance.

'I hope Dance Art isn't competing,' I heard Riley say to Ashley.

'You don't need to worry about that,' said Ashley. 'Jazz Groove is beneath them. They only compete in the big competitions to match their big heads.'

'Sometimes it's good to practise with the smaller comps, so when it comes to the big ones you're prepared,' said Paige.

'I thought it was your mum who made you enter all those comps,' said Riley to Paige.

'That too,' said Paige, with a tiny grin.

'You know, one day your mum's going to jump on the stage and do the dance instead of you,' Riley said.

'If she wins, at least it'll be in your name,' said Ashley.

'Maybe she and Jasmine can do a duet together,' said Riley.

Great. Jasmine. My number one competition. I'd forgotten about her. My stomach did a somersault and I began to feel sick.

'Come on, girls,' said Jay, coming up behind us and ruffling our hair. 'You here to talk or you here to dance?'

Paige blushed.

'Lucky I haven't done my hair yet,' sassed Riley.

Jay pushed open the doors. My stomach did an even bigger somersault. There were some girls inside already, warming up or standing around, looking like they meant business. They were about our age.

I glanced around at the studio jackets everyone was wearing. Rhythmics Dance – no competition there. Jessica Lee Dancers – a couple of really amazing soloists who always placed at competitions, but they were in the older age categories. Isolation Dance School was also there – they could pose some threat in the group dance, but I felt my solo jazz title was secure.

That's when I saw that dreaded gold and blue jacket.

Dance Art Academy.

'Dance Art *are* here!' I exclaimed.

Ashley glanced around and then quietly moved behind Riley.

'Hi Indianna, hi Daisy,' said Jasmine, pushing her way to the front and up to the Dance Art girls.

Jasmine always tries to suck up to Dance Art. It's pretty obvious that it's her dream to wear the blue and gold. I don't know why she didn't switch studios years ago.

'Hi,' they said, not very nicely.

Indianna had glossy brown curls and pouty red lips that had forgotten how to smile. Daisy is Japanese, I think, and really pretty. It's a shame her personality doesn't match her looks.

'I didn't see you at school yesterday,' said Jasmine. She goes to this big rich private school where most of the Dance Art girls go.

'We took the day off to practise,' said Indianna. She had a sour look on her face, like Jasmine was breathing lemons at her or something.

'Are you doing solos?' asked Jasmine. For a moment I thought I saw a flicker of fear on her face.

'No way,' said Daisy. 'We wouldn't do solos in a competition like *this*.'

'Probably because you'd lose,' said Riley, quietly enough to be loud.

'We're just here for the group dance, so we can practise for the big competitions.'

'That's cool,' said Jasmine.

'We saw *you're* doing a solo,' said Indianna.

'Well, um, yeah, er, just for practice.' Jasmine started fiddling with her hair.

‘Well then,’ said Indianna, who now looked like Jasmine had just squashed the lemons all over her face, ‘shouldn’t you go and practise and stop talking to us?’ She grabbed Daisy’s arm and stalked off. They didn’t even look at Ashley.

Wow, and I thought Jasmine was bad.

‘It was great to see you again,’ Ashley said sarcastically.

I thought about seeing if Jasmine was okay, but when I walked into the dressing room she was waiting for me.

‘I hope you’ll be happy with second place,’ she said. There was no fake smile full of bright white teeth this time. Only mean lemony eyes.

Oh, gosh. Forget about somersaults. Now my stomach had face-planted on the floor.

Chapter Fifteen

Backstage was crazy. In the long rectangular room there were sequins and bobby pins scattered everywhere, stockings and leotards hanging from the ceiling, and girls running around with make-up brushes in their hands, calling out for their mums to finish their lipstick.

My mum wasn't backstage. She rarely is. She's pretty busy because she keeps taking on

new personal training clients at the gym and she's also just started the new yoga program. So she doesn't just teach the classes, she does all this fundraising and runs 'healthy eating' workshops. She's pretty sporty. Dad always says she puts him to shame. I reckon I get my athletic ability from her.

Mum always makes it for all my performances, though, even if she's often late, with Lucas hanging off her arm pretending to be a dinosaur. That happened once, in a silent theatre full of people. 'Theatrical talent must run in the family, Mrs Irvin,' Jay had joked. Mum just did her Mum smile.

I went to put my make-up case on the dressing table, but Jasmine's mum held out her hand. Her fingernails looked like angry red talons. 'Not there, Eleanor sweetie, this is Jasmine's corner,' Mrs de Lacy said. Her smile was even brighter and whiter than Jasmine's.

'Oh sorry,' I said, but I wasn't. I'm glad Mum didn't hear my tone of voice – she has this thing about voice tones, and I definitely wasn't using my polite one.

'You can come over here, babe,' called out Paige's mum. 'The lights are better here, anyway.' Under her breath she muttered, 'How ridiculous.' Mrs Montreal was sweeping Paige's hair back into a high, bouncy ponytail.

'Ow, Mum, that's too tight!' Paige complained. Her blonde curls were exploding out of the hair band. If there was a first prize for prettiest, bounciest hair, Paige would win.

'Nonsense, Paigey,' said Mrs Montreal. 'Now fluff it up. Are you right with your make-up? I'll get started on Ellie's hair.'

I sat in the chair while Mrs Montreal swept my hair into an equally tight ponytail – so tight, in fact, that I think my hairline got moved back a few centimetres. Then she began winding it around the curling wand.

I love my hair curly. It's wavy naturally, but when it's in ringlet curls I feel like a celebrity. After a competition I try to leave it like that for as long as possible, until Mum yells at me to have a shower because she could 'fry chips on my head'. Whatever that means.

'Where's my dress, where's my dress?' Tove yelled. 'Has anyone seen it?'

'What colour is it?'

'Did you bring it?'

'I think I saw it near the box of pins!'

In another corner of the room, Bethany was complaining that her hairpiece (she had to wear a fake ponytail because her hair was too short) didn't match the colour of her real hair.

Next to me, Serah was almost in tears because her tulle underlay had ripped and her mum hadn't done her eyeliner right. 'Ten-year-old girls shouldn't have to wear make-up anyway,' grumbled her mum.

She was wrong. Make-up really brings out your features on stage. Sometimes the bright lights can swallow your face. Not actually swallow them, but really wash you out. And because when you dance your face should express the emotion your body's making – it's a pretty big part of the performance.

I was fixing my lipstick (Mrs Montreal had done all the hard stuff, like the false eyelashes) when Ashley slunk over to my side. She looked really worried.

'Hey Ellie,' she said, 'when do we start the warm-up?'

'The what?' I asked.

'The group warm-up,' Ashley said, fiddling with her ponytail. 'At Dance Art we always did a group warm-up together.'

'Oh,' I said. 'We don't do that at Silver Shoes. Everyone knows to prepare in their own time.' I pointed to where Riley and Paige were stretching out in any available space, under the costumes hanging down from the ceiling. Well, I should say Riley was stretching and Paige was trying to swat away her mum, who was 'helping' her down into a back twist.

'Sorry,' said Ashley. 'I didn't know. I better start now then. Thanks.' She scuttled over to a space on the floor. She looked so nervous that I realised how scary it would be, to dance against your old school. Before now I'd thought that Ashley might try to ruin our dance on purpose because she was still loyal to Dance Art, but now I saw that she really wanted to do well.

I couldn't just leave her. At Silver Shoes we stuck together.

'Room for me?' I asked Ashley, taking a seat. 'You want to go over the dance in a bit?'

She smiled at me so warmly I almost didn't care that I was competing against her in the solo section.

Almost.

Chapter Sixteen

The Silver Shoes dance troupe was huddled on the side of the stage, watching the group before us. I looked around at the other girls, with our big eyelashes, bouncy hair and rainbow dresses. We all looked fabulous but a little queasy, because in a minute that would be us, waiting behind the curtain.

I love this moment. Sure, I was nervous but I was also excited. I forgot how annoying

Jasmine was, or that Ashley had waltzed into *my* dance studio and tried to show me up. We were just the Silver Shoes team, about to go on stage together. It was thrilling. I grabbed onto Paige's arm and squeezed. Her curls almost whipped me in the face as she turned around to grin.

The troupe before us finished to a big clap. It was Rhythmics Dance Studio – they'd danced okay but they did the same moves you see at every dance comp. Where Silver Shoes stands out (and why I think we are the BEST studio!) is our choreography – it's amazing, unique and fun. Our teachers, especially Miss Caroline, choose the best, catchiest songs and none of our dances ever looks the same.

Silver Shoes has the wow factor. That's why I love dancing here. That's why I would never go to Dance Art. And that's probably why Ashley had switched.

One girl was a mess as she ran off the stage. She was gasping, 'I forgot, I forgot,' and her friend was trying to give her a running hug. Hugs don't really help in a situation like that. It's a terrible feeling when you forget what's supposed to come next. It's embarrassing *and* heartbreaking, because you know you've ruined your one big chance.

Jasmine huddled us together once the Rhythmics girls were out of the wings. 'Let's do it, Silver Shoes,' she whispered. I didn't even mind that she was taking charge. The girls probably had enough of me bossing them around anyway.

The adjudicator rang the bell and Silver Shoes were announced. We had ten seconds to get on stage and in position before the curtain opened. I ran out to where I was supposed to start.

Oh, that's right, at the centre front. Take that, Jasmine.

I got down into my front split and held out my arms for Riley. The opening of the song had our partners running on and lifting us up into a straddle jump – Miss Caroline likes to start dances with a bang.

Oh my god. The moment while I waited for that curtain to open felt like *forever*. I had to swallow several times just to stop my breakfast coming up.

But then the curtains opened.

And the music began.

Riley ran on stage and I could feel her reaching for my hands. All her excitement and energy passed from her palm to mine. And then I wasn't nervous anymore. I was just ready.

The funny thing about group dances is that they never feel long enough. When I was up there, getting thrown about by Riley, clapping and kicking at the head of the group, I could have danced forever. I didn't want 'You Can't Stop the Beat' to end.

Miss Caroline really had picked the best eight dancers in our jazz class. From the corner of my eye I could see everyone, and there was barely an arm or leg out of place. A couple of sickled feet, maybe. But that was the worst it got.

All too soon we were about to finish. Four of us cartwheeled through the gaps made by the other girls, then they front-aerialed through us, and we went on like that three more times until we all stag-leaped in the air, turned, and landed in our final pose.

There was a moment of silence and then one person clapped, followed by the whole theatre, with a fair few whistles and whoops as well. The curtain whooshed closed and it was just us again, our chests going up and down like the beat was trapped inside.

Chapter Seventeen

We won, of course. I knew we would.

The adjudicating was held right after our section. The judge said Silver Shoes was the standout, and that she 'did not, indeed, want to stop the beat'. It was so great, and I was so happy for Miss Caroline. Dance Art only got an honourable mention. I bet Ashley was happy about that. Looks like they needed to do a bit more 'practising' for the 'bigger' competitions.

I couldn't celebrate for too long, though. I had to focus and get ready for my solo. I wanted to make the wins two out of two.

My solo was the last out of ten. In some ways it's good to be last. It means you can watch everyone else and study the competition and know just what you have to beat. But it also means your nerves build up, big time.

My nerves were obsessed with the 'what'. What if I forgot the steps? What if there was someone important out there, watching? What if I was doing a leap and I threw up, mid-stride? Vomit on a talent scout's face is no way to impress them.

Ashley was first up, which meant bam, she could get her dance out of the way and just relax.

I stood with her side-stage while she was waiting to go on. She was going over her dance in miniature, in the gap between the wings. You know when you see a dancer and they look sort of zoned out but also like they're having a furious physical argument with themselves? They're usually going over choreography. It's actually really calming right before you go on.

When Ash was announced, she looked like she might run away. But I gave her the Silver Shoes hug and as soon as she strutted onto the stage, you would never have guessed she'd been a mess only five seconds ago.

Watching Ash dance was pure happiness. She eased into the steps like the music was looking for her. Miss Caroline had choreographed her dance to Beyoncé's 'Crazy in Love' and she hit all her steps with so much attitude. The dance didn't have as many technical aspects as mine, and I thought that might go against her. But the way she was sashaying across the stage in her sparkly red pants, you could tell the adjudicator would score her highly.

'You did so great, Ash,' I whispered when she came offstage. Her face was all bright and flushed and she looked in love with dancing. I know the feeling. I gave her another hug. Sure, I'd been a bit of a cow about Ashley, but I know good dancing when I see it. And Ash was an awesome dancer.

I went backstage to warm up and go over my solo. I like to have some me-time before I go on stage. I'm not like Riley or Tove, who can sit around and chat until the minute they go on. I need to focus. And to stay away from everyone in case I throw up.

It's not all glitter and sequins, you know.

'Ellie,' someone hissed at me. I looked up from my moves and realised I'd lost track of time. Paige was waving at me. 'Jasmine's on now! You're next!'

Gosh. Imagine after all this and I missed my cue. I gave Paige a quick hug and then snuck side-stage. I wasn't going to, because I didn't want to watch Jasmine and get put off. But I got too curious in the end.

Jasmine was in control the moment she burst on stage. And I mean burst. She came leaping, jumping and twirling like she wanted to shake the audience from their seats.

And she did. She was perfect. It's not hard to see why Jasmine is my number one rival. She has such beautiful classical lines, which makes her transitions between steps flawless. She was, to put it simply, just wow. And I couldn't even blame it on her choreography being a little too contemporary-based (which her jazz routines sometimes are). This was a whole new dance, and it was almost as jazzy as mine.

After she finished, the applause was so loud it was like there was a whole other hidden audience cheering for her. But when I heard it, something strange happened – I got in the dance zone. All my vomity, nervous, excited feelings vanished. And the only thing left was determination.

I had to get more applause than Jasmine.

The bell rang, my number was called, and I walked out on to the stage.

Chapter Eighteen

How do I explain the feeling when I have a solo, and the stage is all mine, and there's only my dancing to fill it? I am what I'm dancing, but at the same time I'm not me. I'm the best version of Ellie I can be.

When I dance, for that moment, nothing else exists.

You know when you wake up from a really good sleep, and there's soft sunshine coming through the gap in your curtains? Or when you come home from school and it's raining, and your mum has baked a cake, and you curl up on the couch to eat it, and the lounge room is all shadowy and dark? Or when you walk into an old theatre, and no one else is around, and you can see the dust swirling on the stage and think that it might be the ghosts of old actors up there, playing around?

That's how I feel when I dance. It's thrilling. It's my inspiration and my motivation all at once.

I was out there with my gorgeous costume, the feathers and the hoop and the big band music. The lights were in my eyes and the audience was a sea of blurry faces. There was a horrible two seconds of silence while I waited in position for the music.

But then it hit. And my arms reacted instantly. Up, down, up, down, turn around.

Kick, drag, kick, drag, pause. Double pirouette, pause, catch the hoop. Breathe.

The start was over. Now I just wanted to entertain the audience.

One of the best things about being on stage in front of an audience is that it makes you add little flourishes that turn a dance into a performance. I'm not talking about adding in whole new moves. I'm talking a flick there, a glance here, a shoulder there. Pulling the audience into the dance with you. I wanted them to feel how it made me feel, being up on stage, dancing. So I pushed my legs a little higher and I arched my back a bit more, and I made sure there was as much care put into my transitions as there was all my featured 'tricks'.

There was one moment when the hoop almost got away from me. But I covered it up by acting as if the hoop was naughty. Then

I grabbed it as I transitioned to my next jump. Not once did I lose energy, or my face sag. I could see people watching me from side-stage, peering out between the curtains, and that put a little lift in my jumps too.

I knew, as I held my final position, and the applause *was* as loud as Jasmine's, that I'd done the best I could possibly do. When you hear people clapping for you it's like they're catching smiles and throwing them up on the stage. I felt like a million bucks.

'Hold Infinity in the palm of your hand,' that poem says. 'And Eternity in an hour.' I don't know if dancers would hold infinity in the palms of their hands – it would probably be more like the soles of their feet. But I was holding it somewhere as I bowed and the audience clapped, and I made my way back into the crush of the side curtains.

Infinity. Eternity. Whatever you want to call it. That's what dancing creates. That's what the magic is on stage.

Chapter Nineteen

Adjudication time! The moment of truth! I wondered if Silver Shoes could take home first, second and third. Would it be me with the tallest trophy?

Miss Caroline was standing at the side of the stage with us. Sometimes when she's side-stage she stares out through the wings and looks all dreamy. I guess she's remembering when she used to dance. But today she just looked very excited for her Silver Shoes girls. Jasmine, Ashley and I each got a squeeze on the arm as we walked out onto the stage to hear the results.

The audience clapped for us again and over all of them I heard Lucas yelling, 'Ellie, Ellie!' I gave him an embarrassed wave and everyone laughed. Then he stood up on the seat, held his arms out like a T-rex, and yelled 'Rawwwrrrrr!' The audience loved it. Geez. It was like he was the one up on stage, not me!

After he'd got the most out of his ten seconds of fame (well, it was cute), the adjudicator said how delighted she was with this section, and what great choices of music and different styles of jazz she'd seen this afternoon. 'Keep working on your technique,' she said, 'and keep up all that wonderful energy.'

She then read out her choice for honourable mention – I secretly crossed my fingers that it wasn't me. There's nothing wrong with getting an HM, of course, but I was really after something a little higher for my solo. I'd worked so hard.

The HM went to a girl from Isolation. We all clapped for her as she collected her ribbon, but my mind was somewhere else.

Three places left. Jasmine. Ashley. Me. I felt sure it would come down to us. I kept my smile big, but I was starting to get tummy somersaults again.

'Third place goes to a performer who was a breath of fresh air; so much fun and such a great understanding of the music – I really enjoyed this performance. Congratulations to competitor number one, Ashley.'

Ashley for third! You could tell she was thrilled. I was actually really happy for her.

But Ashley getting third meant there were now only two places left. I was so busy thinking about it that I didn't even realise the adjudicator had started speaking again. I only tuned in when I heard her say, 'What a performer, competitor number ten, Eleanor!'

That was me! I looked over at the wings and there was the presenter, holding out my trophy. My brain clicked back into the present and I curtsied and dashed over to receive it. But what was it? Second or first? I almost didn't want to look.

But I did.

Second.

I'd come second.

And when I looked up again, Jasmine was rushing over to receive her first-place trophy.

Jasmine had won.

Jasmine, who threw a clown nose at me, and whispered mean things in class, and flashed her bright white teeth whenever Miss Caroline gave her a compliment (which was always).

For a moment I felt absolutely crushed.

But only for a moment.

Because Jasmine deserved to get first. She had danced brilliantly. It would have been nice if her personality was as brilliant as her dancing, but I guess you can't have it all.

And I was still the second-best jazz dancer in my age group. I'd danced in front of all these people, and it was amazing. And when I looked out into the audience, Lucas was jumping up and down in his chair and Mum was standing and clapping with a huge smile on her face. And Paige and Miss Caroline were waiting in the wings with the biggest, warmest hugs.

And I was part of Silver Shoes, the best dance school ever.

Full name: Eleanor Charlotte Irvin
Nicknames: Elle, Ellie
Age: 10
Favourite dance styles: Jazz & Broadway
Best friend: Paige
Family: Mum, Dad, and my five-year-old brother, Lucas
Favourite colour: Pink
Favourite food: Milkshakes, pancakes and jelly snakes
Favourite school subjects: Music and creative writing (why don't they have dance as a subject!)

Hobbies: Singing, dancing, acting, watching dance movies, fashion, writing stories, putting on shows (even if only Lucas watches them!)

What I want to be when I grow up: A dancer, of course! Or a famous choreographer.

Best dancing moment: When I won the whole school talent show in Grade One. Or the first musical I ever saw (*42nd Street*). Or maybe when I beat Jasmine in the Under 8s Dancefest Competition. Actually, pretty much every time I dance!

Things I love: Dancing, being on stage, musical theatre, the applause after a performance, my pink jazz boots, anything sparkly, pop music, playing dinosaurs with Lucas, my friends, and whenever Jasmine gets in trouble

How to do a Perfect Grand Jeté

A grand jeté is a leap from one leg to the other where one leg extends straight out in front and the other straight out behind. Follow the movements in the illustrations below, from left to right, to complete a grand jeté that looks graceful and effortless.

Tips

- Try to create an arc with your jump. A grand jeté should go up and over, not up and down.
- Keep your head up and your gaze forward. This will help you jump higher and land smoothly.

Glossary

Hi everyone! Here are some jazz dance terms – there are heaps more, though! You might like to search on the internet for a 'dance glossary', which will tell you a lot more about all the cool moves we do in class. I also love YouTube-ing them so I know exactly how they're done.

Love, Ellie

adjudicator the person who judges a dance competition. He or she uses a points system to rate dancers on things such as skill, performance quality, difficulty and presentation.

aerial a cartwheel performed without your hands on the floor

arabesque to position yourself on one leg, with the other leg raised straight behind your body at 90 degrees or higher

attitude a pose where one leg is raised in back or in front with your knee bent and toe pointed. Usually you raise one arm too.

axle jump a turning jump where you take off and land on the same foot, keeping your body upright and tucking your right knee into your chest as you turn

barre a bar at waist level used for support during warm-up exercises

chassé a travelling or connecting three-step pattern that is basically a gliding gallop where the same foot always leads

choreographer the 'designer' of a dance routine. Choreography is all the moves,

sequences, patterns and form that make up a dance.

fouette a whipping move, where one leg opens and closes quickly from second to passé, allowing you to turn on your other leg. Usually done on the spot.

front aerial a front walkover without using hands for support; different from a side aerial, which is a cartwheel without using hands for support

grande jeté to leap from one leg to the other where one leg extends straight out in front and the other straight out behind

passé a turned-out position, where one leg makes a triangular shape as the inside toe passes or touches just below the kneecap of the supporting leg; can be either to the front or to the side

pirouette a turn performed on one foot, on the spot

plié to bend your knees in any of the five positions, with your body upright

pointe position on the tips of your toes

sickled when you point your feet but instead of making a straight line from your leg through to your foot, your ankle rolls inward

side split kick when you kick your leg upward to the side while standing on one foot, aiming for a straddle split in the air

side split leap you can also call this a straddle leap, where you jeté but to the side in a straddle position

splits a physical position where your legs are in line with each other and stretched out in opposite directions. You can straddle split or front split.

stag leap a high leap or jump in a split but with both legs in a bent (attitude) position. Your arms should be straight up in the air and your body squared to the front.

straddle jump to jump into the side splits from a standing position

switch leaps a jeté but where you swing one leg forward and then back, lifting into a split leap, so your legs 'switch' places in the air. Also called a scissor leap.

swizzle an acro move performed with two people, where the person standing up lets the other person 'fall' towards the floor, but swoops them up and around

transition the movement, passage or change that you use to get from step to step

About the Author

Samantha-Ellen Bound has been an actor, dancer, teacher, choreographer, author, bookseller, scriptwriter and many other things besides. She has published and won prizes for her short stories and scripts, but children's books are where her heart lies. Dancing is one of her most favourite things in the whole world. She splits her time between Tasmania, Melbourne, and living in her own head.

OUT NOW!

LOOK OUT FOR THE NEXT
SILVER SHOES BOOKS

Breaking Pointe

AND

Dance Till You Drop

AVAILABLE APRIL 2015